' "I'll teach you to be brav
All looked up. Scales was
wov............ly in and out of the
thorny branches, not minding the spikes a
bit. He reached down and hauled them up
one by one. There was a scratchy feeling, a
tangly feeling, then –

"Here we are," cried Scales cheerfully.
"Spring on Magic Mountain!" ' '

Sam and his friends are so disappointed
when they return to school only to find
that they won't be seeing Scales, the
friendly young dragon. Their teacher, Miss
Green, has moved Scales' cave to a
stockroom and Class 4 are now supposed
to get enthusiastic about a computer
instead.

But with the coming of spring, Scales
wakes up and is soon an important
member of the class again, leading Sam
and his friends to Magic Mountain for
some exciting and extraordinary
adventures.

June Counsel has written several books
for children, including DRAGON IN
CLASS 4, the first book about Scales.

Also by June Counsel, and published by
Corgi Yearling Books:

DRAGON IN CLASS 4
A DRAGON IN SUMMER
DRAGON IN TOP CLASS

Also by June Counsel, published by
Picture Corgi Books:

BUT MARTIN!

DRAGON
IN
SPRING-TERM

JUNE COUNSEL

Illustrated by Jill Bennett

YEARLING BOOKS

DRAGON IN SPRING-TERM
A CORGI YEARLING BOOK 0 440 86209 4

Originally published in Great Britain by
Faber and Faber Ltd

PRINTING HISTORY
Faber and Faber edition published 1988
Yearling edition published 1989
Reprinted 1991, 1992
Reissued 1996

This book is set in 14/16pt Century textbook
by Colset Private Limited, Singapore.

Yearling Books are published by Transworld Publishers Ltd,
61–63 Uxbridge Road, Ealing, London W5 5SA,
in Australia by Transworld Publishers (Australia) Pty Ltd,
15–25 Helles Avenue, Moorebank, NSW 2170,
and in New Zealand by Transworld Publishers (NZ) Ltd,
3 William Pickering Drive, Albany, Auckland.

Printed and bound in Great Britain by
Cox & Wyman Ltd, Reading, Berkshire

To Alan

Contents

1 New Beginnings

Swinging along the lane to school on a jolly January morning, Sam felt bouncy with joy. He stopped at the Rec to look at the baby swings where he had first seen Scales, the little dragon, tangled up in the bars, but there was nothing in the baby swings now except snow, because Scales was hibernating in the cave Class 4 had made for him. But he'll be waking soon, thought Sam joyfully, because this is Spring-term and dragons wake in the spring.

It *was* the spring term, but nowhere near spring. Snow lay about, bright and sparkling, not giving an inch, though the sun was shining.

'It's waiting for more to fall,' said Miss Green, when they were all seated. 'That's what they say when snow hangs about. Well, how are you all?'

New was how they all were. Weefy had a new jumper with SAVE THE WHALE on, which his mum had knitted, Sebastian had a new bow tie, Christopher had a new book, Sam showed his new fluorescent felt-tip pens which wrote in colours like light. Ivy Grubb had so many new things it took till playtime to show them all. Little Tina had new patches on her old frock and Billy Bottom had new stains on his dirty sweater. Miss Green had a new handbag.

'Has no one noticed we have something new in the classroom?' cried Miss Green.

The chatter stopped. All heads turned.

'In the corner,' exclaimed Miss Green. 'My gracious me, look!'

All eyes looked.

'It's a computer,' cried clever Christopher, whose father taught at the Tech.

'It came at the end of last term,' explained Miss Green, 'but there was

so much going on, that I thought we'd have it new this term.'

'What's it do?' cried Dinny Delmont.

'Lovely things,' said Miss Green. 'You can do maths on it, spelling, drawing and, if you're good, you can play games on it.'

'But that's where Scales' cave was,' said Sam suddenly. He looked round for the Measuring Table which had held Scales' cave last term, but the Measuring Table was back at its old job. There was not a corner nor a space left for Scales in the whole classroom.

'Is he going to have to stay in the bay?' he asked anxiously.

For Scales and his cave had been shoved into the bay at the end of last term and Scales had hated it. The bay was through an archway. It was really a small room built on to the classroom. The sink was there and the big chest that held the different drawing papers. It was sunny and peaceful, and lonely.

But Miss Green didn't answer. 'Now then,' she said, 'have you all written your thank-you letters?'

'Yes,' said Sebastian smugly, 'I wrote all mine on Boxing Day.'

'I wrote an unthank-you one,' said Weefy, that odd boy, 'but my mum wouldn't let me send it.'

'Oh, Weefy!'

'Well, my double-nan sent me a pull-along woolly dog on wheels as if I were a baby.'

'Your great-grandmother can't help being old and forgetful,' said Miss Green. 'She spent time, money and energy on buying it. You should thank her for that. Let's all write a thank-you letter for a present that wasn't quite what we wanted and see how kind we can be without being untruthful.'

She wrote on the blackboard:

Dear Aunt Mary,
Thank you for the pair of mittens you knitted for me. They were

rather big. I think you must have got so excited watching television that you forgot to stop! I have cut off the tops of the thumbs and unpicked a bit of the sides and now I have a splendid pair of tea cosies, and you know how much I like hot tea! So thank you very much.

Love from Miss Green

She looked thoughtfully at Tina and Billy. Tina might be poor, but she had plenty of love, but Billy – Billy didn't look as though he was getting much of anything just now.

'Tina and Billy, you two shall be the first to use the new computer. Sit beside me and I'll show you what to do. The rest of you make up a thank-you letter for something you didn't like and remember, no lies!'

Class 4 began to write. Weefy wrote, 'Dear Nan, Thank you for my pull-along woolly dog on wheels. I am going to put Dracula teeth on him to scare Lumpy Custard.' Lumpy Custard was Weefy's cat, a yellow tom with a matted coat, whom nothing scared.

Ivy Grubb began making a list of all her presents. 'I'm up to twenty-two,' she announced, 'and I'm still not finished.'

Sam alone did not write. His mind was full of Scales.

'Miss Green,' he asked, 'aren't we going to have Scales in the classroom? He doesn't like being in the bay.'

'Sam,' called Miss Green from the computer, 'we aren't even going to have him in the bay. Mr Duffy and I have put his cave in the stockroom. We shall use it again some day, I expect.'

'But . . .' stammered Sam.

'Scales was last term,' said Miss Green firmly. 'He was fun and we loved him, but this is a new term and we do new things.'

There was a knock on the door and Miss Barley put her head round.

'Miss Green,' she whispered.

Miss Green went swiftly out of the room and closed the door behind her. Sam felt desolate. All the bounce went out of him. No Scales? Class 4 without Scales?

'Don't worry, Sam,' said Weefy, drawing a fearsome woolly dog with Dracula teeth. 'Scales is magic. He won't stay in the stockroom.'

Miss Green popped her head round the door. 'Class 4, I'm just going up the corridor with Miss Barley for a few minutes. Finish your thank-you letters and draw a picture at the end.' She saw Sam's miserable face. 'Sam, you go over to Billy and Tina and play a game on the computer with them.'

Sam went lumpily over to the computer, thinking of Scales.

'You are sad,' said tiny Tina. 'We will play a game to cheer you up.' She shot a disc in. 'You start, Sam.'

Sam looked moodily down at the keys, then caught his breath. Billy looked and cried, 'Whoops, Sam!'

Tina saw, and shook Sam. 'It is for you, for you, from Scales, press it, Sam!'

For amongst the white keys, one had suddenly turned green, not a plastic green, but a strange, pulsing green, on off, on off, on off, that seemed almost to sing. Trembling, Sam put his finger on it. A tiny electric shock ran up to his elbow. He pressed. At once the screen began to print in the flickering green letters.

Dear Sam,
Thank you for the tail warmer. I didn't really want one, so I gave it to my silly cousins. Half of them get into it and the rest pull them along. Then they change over. It doesn't do your mum's knitting any good, but they love it and I DON'T HAVE TO PLAY WITH THEM, so thank you very much.
  Love from Scales X X O

'What's X X O mean?' asked Billy.
'Kiss, kiss, hug,' said Sam, 'you put

it at the end of letters. Bill, this is terrif, this means Scales is awake. Even if he isn't *here*, he's awake.'

'Our dear Scales,' cried little Tina, clapping her hands, while Billy's smile stretched from ear to ear.

'Hey up!' he cried. 'Look.'

The letters had vanished and the magic green was hopping from key to key. At once their excited fingers followed it and, as they pressed, a picture began to form on the screen.

'You others,' cried Billy, 'come here. Scales is drawing a picture.'

With a rush Class 4 put down its pencils and crowded round the computer.

'It's the cave on Magic Mountain! There's all Scales' silly cousins. There's Billy, stuffing himself with a rock cake. Sam's there with you, and Tina. Scales is drawing a party!'

'It's not fair,' grumbled Ivy Grubb, as she watched, 'why only Sam and Tina and Billy? Why doesn't Scales put me in? I should like a rock cake.'

The door opened. Miss Green came in. The picture vanished. Class 4 scuttled back to its place.

'Thank-you letters on my desk, please. Ivy, you collect them. Eat your lunch, children, the bell is just going. Did you enjoy the computer, Sam?'

'Yes,' smiled Sam.

'Good lad, I thought you would. New things are fun. There's the bell now, everyone out.' And Miss Green sailed off to the staffroom with her new handbag over her arm. Sam went quickly over to the computer. A faint tinge of green still pulsed on one of the keys. He pressed it and began to type.

Dear Scales,
Miss has locked you in the stockroom because we did you last term. This is a new term and we are going to do new things.
    Love
      Sam

He pressed the return key and waited. Three giant words came marching on to the screen and stood there, flashing on off, on off, on off, for a full half minute:

SO AM I

2 Scales Comes Nearer

Miss Green was so pleased with the thank-you letters that she pinned them up in the corridor. Miss Barley read them and smiled till she came to one in the middle.

' "Dear Miss Green," ' she read. ' "Thank you for putting my cave in the stockroom. It isn't quite what I wanted, but I like having paper and crayons around me. When I am bored

I shall be able to draw. Love from Scales." Who wrote that?'

Miss Green went pink and took the letter down quickly.

'Class 4 are upset because I've put Scales' cave in the stockroom and won't allow him in this term, but it is a new term and we must do new things.'

'Quite right,' nodded Miss Barley. 'But his cave was very beautiful. Why don't you use it in your spring work? Tell them the story of Persephone. She could come out of the cave.'

So Miss Green told Class 4 about Persephone, but she didn't bring Scales' cave out of the stockroom. The next day Christopher brought his new book to school.

'It's got that story you were telling us in, Miss,' he said.

Weefy stared at the title. 'Percy *phone*?' he frowned.

'*Per-sef-on-ee*,' explained Christopher. 'It's Greek. Here she is picking flowers. Here's the earth opening up and King Hades, *Hay-dees*, rushing up to take her away. Here they are in his gloomy underworld, and here's her mother come to beg him for her. And here she is at the end, coming up into the light and all the flowers beginning to bloom.'

'It is a beautiful story, like spring coming after winter,' said Italian Tina dreamily.

So thought all Class 4 and they played Persephone in the playground. Tina was Persephone and Christopher was King Hades, and Ivy Grubb was Persephone's mum, Demeter ('De-*mee*-ter,' said Christopher fiercely). Tina got rather torn about, because Christopher wouldn't let go of her, neither would Ivy. Miss Green, who was on playground duty, stopped the tug-of-war.

'That's enough,' she said. 'Poor Persephone, she'll never come if you tear her to bits.'

'I wish Per-sef would come hopping down those gardens and cheer them up,' said Weefy, looking at the

gardens beyond the railings, where sad, black snowmen were dwindling daily, their carrot noses withering at their feet.

PE cheered Class 4 up, and afterwards Miss Green said Christopher's table could go to the library and Christopher could read the story of Persephone to them out of his book.

The library was in the main corridor. It had books on easy-to-reach shelves, carpet on the floor and comfortable chairs. Some of the chairs they moved so that the rabbit and guinea pig who lived in a cage further up the corridor could come down and listen. Christopher was a super reader. Words he didn't know, he guessed, words he couldn't guess he left out, so the story sailed on with never a break and carried them with it. Some of Class 5 who were playing with the big bricks further down stole up to listen.

'Can we bring our hamster?' they whispered.

'Yes,' said Christopher and went on reading.

So Class 5 went back, asked permission, and came back with Toffee. The rabbit and guinea pig listened in a fidgety way, but Toffee sat in a Class 5 lap and never moved. When the dinner bell went, it was like waking out of a dream.

'I was there,' sighed Tina. 'I felt so sad for Demeter looking and looking and calling for Persephone.'

'What made her go looking for her?' asked Billy.

'She missed her,' said Christopher, closing the book.

That afternoon a bad-tempered rain

began to batter on the windows.

'Indoor play again,' sighed Miss Green as the bell went. 'Dish out the comics, Sam.'

Then she took the cup of tea Jenny the Helper brought her and went to patrol the corridors.

'Hullo,' said Class 5, suddenly appearing before Sam and Billy. 'We've brought Toffee to see you.'

Billy stretched out and took Toffee and put her up his jumper, and the five Class 5, who had listened to the story, laughed at her scrabbling.

'She likes you, Billy.'

'Let's show Toffee our computer,' suggested Sam and led them over to the computer, where Billy put Toffee gently on the keys.

'Scales sent a message on the computer yesterday,' Sam told Class 5. He was feeling suddenly excited, as though he wanted to dance and skip.

'Ooh,' breathed Class 5, impressed, and stared at the screen, but nothing came on. It was a most unmagical day and so dark it might have been evening outside.

Then Toffee squeaked, Class 5 jumped and Sam and Billy gasped as a great green PLEASE shot on to the screen and stayed there pulsing vehemently, and vehemently, as Christopher would say, means very, very strongly. Then it vanished and Toffee at once began to move carefully about on the keys. More letters came on, but just ordinary ones that spelt out ALL RIGHT. Then the screen cleared, Toffee got off the computer and Class 5 picked her up.

'Who's a clever hamster then?' they cooed and carried her back to their classroom, leaving Sam and Billy agog.

'Scales has asked her to do something,' Sam said excitedly.

'And Toffee's said she will,' nodded Billy, and they both tingled all over.

The week went on, the weather got worse, bad things happened. Vandals broke into the Juniors, someone heaved a brick through Class 1's window, and Toffee went missing.

'Oh dear,' said Miss Green as she read the sad little note Class 5 brought round. ' "Our hamster is missing. Please could you look for her. She likes dark corners and warm places." Let's all have a quick look, Class 4.'

Class 4 looked in its trays, Miss Green pulled out her desk drawers and gave a cry.

'My Magic Markers are gone!'

Class 4 looked up. Billy dropped his tray.

'I must report this to Miss Barley,' said Miss Green, looking troubled, and left the room.

'Miss should lock her drawers always,' said smug Sebastian, 'and not just when she's got money in them.'

'You haven't got them up your jumper, have you, Billy?' asked Ivy Grubb, tossing her ringlets.

Billy's face flamed. He was just

swinging up his tray to bonk it down on Ivy's head when Miss Green came in.

'Stop that, Billy. Now, class, if *any* of you know *any*thing about this matter, you must tell me. Promise?'

Class 4 looked at her with solemn eyes and promised, except Billy who had his head down and was muttering.

'Good. Now then, Billy, Sam and Dinny, I want you to help me get the stiff paper out of the stockroom, because Miss Barley has asked *us* to do the library picture, and we need the special stiff paper for that.'

So the three followed her up the corridor, Sam and Dinny chattering, Billy head down, face red, fists clenched, muttering.

Miss Green unlocked the stockroom and stared aghast.

'It's *stuffed*,' she gasped, 'and, of course, what we want is right at the back.'

It was, too. Tall rolls of stiff paper

in brilliant colours stood at the back like a row of pillars. Skinny Dinny Delmont and unskinny Miss Green wriggled through, heaved up one of the heavy rolls and passed it out to big strong Billy and fairly strong Sam.

'Gracious,' cried Miss Green, 'what have we here?'

For behind the row of paper pillars was a mound of torn-up paper. Dinny dropped to her knees and went squirming forward.

'It's Scales' cave,' she shrilled. 'There's all torn-up paper in it and . . .'

'Careful,' warned Miss Green, 'don't put your hand in. Let's get it out.'

That was a puffing job! Two more heavy rolls had to be lifted out, and then Scales' dusty cave, full most mysteriously of torn-up paper.

'Now,' panted Miss Green, 'Sam, you and Dinny carry it gently down to Class 5 who I think will be glad to see

it. Billy, my man of muscle, you stay with me, please, and help me get these pillars back, because otherwise I shall go pop!'

So Sam and Dinny carried Scales' cave carefully down the corridor and knocked at the Class 5 door, and Class 5 put its hand in and joyfully drew out a sleepy Toffee.

'Oh, you bad little hamster,' they cried, loving her, 'did you go and make a nest in the stockroom then?'

Dinny and Sam took Scales' cave through into their bay, swept the paper out of it, and put it under the table by the window. Then they carefully arranged a chair or two in front of it.

'Your cave's ready, Scales,' Sam whispered into the dark mouth. 'It's out of the stockroom. Toffee planned it.'

'We've swept it out,' breathed Dinny beside him. 'It's clean.'

Then they went into the classroom just as Miss Green and Billy staggered in, their arms full of exciting paper. Their faces were red with exertion and bright with happiness.

'Right,' called Miss Green, 'we're going to start the library picture *now*. What shall it be?'

'A mountain, and a cave, snow melting, the earth opening, flowers coming up . . .' called Class 4.

'The story of Persephone,' nodded Miss Green, smiling. 'Good. The coming of spring.'

The coming of *Scales*, thought Sam and his heart leaped.

3 The Freezing White Fog

Next day at breakfast Sam told his
mother about Scales' cave.

'We've got it back in the bay,' he
said jubilantly, 'and soon he'll wake
up and be with us.'

'He won't wake up yet,' said
his mother. 'Look at the weather!
If he's sensible he'll sleep till
spring.' Outside the window it was
white, but not with snow, with

freezing fog, with freezing white fog.

Walking along the lane was like walking in ghost-land. Sounds were muffled, shapes were shrouded. Miss Barley stood like a wraith in the yard calling the children to come straight in although the bell hadn't gone. Sam went to Scales' cave and knelt down by it. The freezing white fog pressed against the window.

'Scales, are you awake?'

He put his hand in. Nothing. He shut his eyes and listened with every cell in his body. Nothing. He stood up, disconsolate. Sebastian came up to him, his bow tie quivering with excitement.

'Sam, Sam, what do you think? It was Billy took the Magic Markers. It was his brothers who broke into the Juniors. It was one of them threw the brick through Class 1's window. His mum's left his dad and they're living on baked beans.'

'How do you know?' asked Sam, scowling. He didn't want to think about Billy. He wanted to think about Scales, but Sebastian bubbled on.

'They sent Billy over to borrow our tin opener, because they'd thrown theirs away by mistake. They don't cook their beans. They put their fingers in the tin and eat them cold.'

Sam felt jollier. His mum never let him put his fingers in the baked bean tin. It sounded a good thing to do. Miss Green came in. The rest of Class 4 straggled in. The bell went. No Billy.

'A news flash before we begin,' said Miss Green. 'The Magic Markers are back. The person who took them has said they're sorry and . . .'

'I know who took them,' interrupted Sebastian.

'I'm sure you do, Sebastian,' said Miss Green. 'Others do, too, I expect, but the matter is closed. I shall keep my drawers locked in future and you must all help me to remember.'

'I bet Billy's brothers made him do

it,' murmured Weefy to Sam. 'They're always on at him to steal.'

Billy had several brothers, who came and went. When they went it was mostly to prison and when they came it was usually to steal.

'Here he is,' cried Sam.

In came Billy, his hair wet with fog, his face red with cold, orange stains round his mouth and orange stains on his jersey and a baked bean clinging to his front. Both knees of his dungarees were split and his scabbed blue knees showed through.

'Oh, Billy, I'm glad to see you,' cried Miss Green. 'You're just in time for Music and Movement. Two lines by the door, everyone, and into the hall.'

In the hall Miss Green switched on the loud-speaker and a man's voice said, 'Today we are going to have a strange adventure. Listen to the music.'

Swirly music came out of the loud-speaker. 'You are going to an alien planet,' said the man. 'Form into fours and build your spaceship. Listen to the building music.'

Sam formed into a four with Weefy, Billy and Christopher, and they built their spaceship.

'Now,' said the man, 'put on your spacesuits, slowly, slowly, climb into your spaceship, slowly, slowly. When the music quickens, press the controls – and off you go!'

'We don't want to go to any boring old planet,' whispered Christopher. 'We'll go to Magic Mountain.'

The music quickened. They pressed the controls. They had lift-off!

'Come back,' cried the loudspeaker man suddenly, 'you're doing it wrong, it's only pretend.'

But it wasn't pretend, and they were doing it right. They were hurtling through the freezing white fog towards Magic Mountain and, suddenly, bonk, with a bump and a bounce they landed, and stepped out.

'Hey,' cried Christopher, 'we can't see a thing!'

For all around them curled the freezing white fog. Nothing but whiteness, till suddenly a great black boot, big as a wheelbarrow, came down and squashed their spaceship flat. A second boot came down.

'Look out!' they shouted. The boot paused, hovered, then trod gently down. A hand the size of a small table came groping after it.

'Oh, oh, it's a giant,' quavered Weefy. 'He'll squash us.'

'Run,' ordered Christopher, when the fog rolled away and they were staring up at a giant, bent double staring at them.

Sam spoke up firmly. 'Please, are we near Scales' cave?'

'That squeak must be its voice,' rumbled the giant, trying to focus his huge eyes on Sam. 'Ah, there it is. A little tiny tiny boy.'

'Can you take us to Scales' cave?'

shouted Christopher. The giant seemed friendly.

He was friendly, but not obliging. 'No, I can't. For why? For because they're all asleep and they've got the old 'un staying with 'em, Scales' gran, and I dursn't wake her, and for because I've got a job to do. I've come to wake the Spring Girl.'

He knelt down and pushed aside a few small trees that grew along the lip of a deep crack in the ground and called down it:

'Come up, Persephone. Please, girl, come up. Come and make the grass grow so the cows will get fat so people will get fat so I will get fat.'

'Do you eat people?' asked Sam, horrified.

'Everybody eats somebody,'

answered the giant. He went on in a gentle roar, 'I've brought presents, Persephone, from everyone.'

He began pushing things into the crack. Such pretty, hopeful things, a bunch of dried flowers, a picture of the sun, a packet of seeds, a necklace made of shells.

'We'll give presents, too,' cried Christopher and took out a handful of brightly coloured animals that he had collected from cornflake packets. Sam gave his king conker, wrinkled now and brown, but still a giant. Weefy took off his Ban the Bomb badge and Billy parted with his favourite bit of string. Christopher wrote on his pad:

'Please Persephone come to Class 4 *soon.*'

The giant took the letter and their presents and dropped them into the dark crack. A sweet, flutey sound stole up.

'Ah,' rumbled the giant, listening, 'that pleased her. She'll see you don't starve.' He began lumbering to his feet. 'I'm going back home now.'

The boys looked at each other. Home? Back? 'But we can't get back home,' blubbered Weefy, 'because you squashed our spaceship.'

They felt suddenly lonely in spite of the giant and cold in spite of their spacesuits.

The giant stooped down again, moving his head about till he saw the squashed spaceship. The freezing white fog came curling back.

'That it? That tiny little thing? Jump on my hand then and I'll take you back. Now which mountain or valley is yours?'

They clambered aboard his broad palm. Weefy collapsed in the hollow,

Sam sat astride a finger, Christopher held on to the thumb. Billy stood upright, balancing himself with outstretched arms. The hand rose slowly up through the freezing white fog.

'Over there,' cried Christopher, consulting his compass, 'eastwards. We live in the fens, where it's flat.'

The giant

s-t-r-e-t-c-h-e-d

his long arm out through the freezing white fog.

Brrr, it was cold. Shiver, it was damp. They could barely see each other. They couldn't see the giant. A gentle bump, the sound of a click. They were in the hall and Miss Green, with her back to them, was switching off the loudspeaker.

'You were a dozy lot,' she was saying, 'I think the fog must have got into you.'

In the classroom, they took their lunch boxes to their table and –

'Our mums have gone mad!' cried

Christopher, staring, for in every lunch box – *double* lunch! *Two* gingerbread squares in Christopher's, *two* healthy apples in Weefy's, *two* packets of crisps in Sam's, and other goodies besides.

'It's a feast!' cried Sam. 'Tuck in, Billy.'

4 Cheer-up Monday

After the freezing fog went, the snow
came back. It lay about in dingy
heaps like old jumble, and the cold
deepened.

'It's freezing in here,' complained
Class 4.

'Give the poor old heating a chance,
it's only Monday,' said Miss Green.

'Mondays are mouldy,' mumbled
Sam.

Billy Bottom said nothing, but drove his pencil savagely through his newsbook.

'My throat's sore,' croaked Ivy Grubb, and gave a prim little cough. At once a chorus of coughs broke out, big coughs, little coughs, spitty coughs, silly coughs.

'Hush!' commanded Miss Green. 'I name this day Cheer-up Monday! We'll make a comic book, funny stories, comic strips, funny recipes, but you must make up your *own* jokes, your *own* recipes, your *own* strip.'

'Great,' cried Christopher. 'We'll do a comic strip.'

'You'll need space,' smiled Miss Green. 'Go in the bay and spread yourselves out.'

So Christopher, Sam, Weefy Buffalo and Billy Bottom went into the bay, spread a sheet of sugar paper on the floor and knelt round it. Christopher began ruling lines.

'I'll rule the squares for the

pictures. I've got a fab idea for a story.'

Trouble was, he had too many ideas. The story kept changing and the others got dizzy listening.

'I'm going to do my own comic strip,' Weefy said at last. 'It's like being in a spin-drier listening to you.'

'Let's start drawing the pictures first and see what happens,' suggested Sam.

Soon all were busy, drawing, writing, colouring, crossing out and starting again, except Billy, who sat hunched and silent, taking no part.

'What's up, Billy?' Sam asked, but Billy only pressed his lips together.

He did not know what was up. He only knew he was down.

'You can start colouring in now, Billy,' said Christopher kindly, but Billy stuck his hands in his pockets.

'He feels humpy,' remarked Weefy. 'Leave him alone. He'll come out of it.'

Whether it was Billy's gloom, or the day's mouldiness, the comic strips became steadily unfunnier and the cartoonists glummer and glummer.

'It's hard work being funny,' grumbled Weefy.

'I don't know how cartoonists do it,' said Christopher sulkily. 'Some cartoonists draw a cartoon every *day*.'

The sugar paper looked as though they were drawing a battle, there were so many crossings-outs, so many confused colours, so many WHAMS, BANGS, POWS and EEEKS! Sam's hands ached with drawing and his head with thinking.

'What we want,' he said sadly, 'is someone with super ideas who *is* fun to start us off.'

The others looked at him quickly. Billy stopped scowling.

'Call him, Sam,' Christopher said urgently. 'Call him by his magic name. We'll put our fingers in our ears so we don't hear.'

'He's hibernating,' Sam said sadly. 'He'll be asleep.'

'Not all the time he won't be,' said Weefy. 'Our tortoise wakes up if it's sunny.'

'Grizzly bears do, too,' said Christopher.

'Go on,' they urged, '*do*.' Billy said nothing, but his eyes begged like a dog's asking for a walk.

Sam felt his heart begin to race. 'All right,' he said, 'block your ears and shut your eyes.'

The others stuffed their fingers in their ears and shut their eyes, so they shouldn't even *see* Sam say the magic name; Sam tensed and quivered.

'Sep-dibby-di-dum!'
he whispered.

A curious sensation, a most odd

feeling, as though the sugar paper was folding itself round them and pulling them through the floor, through darkness, till, bump, their bottoms banged on a sandy floor, the sugar paper unfolded, and

'SCALES!'

they shouted.

Scales it was, in his secret drawing place with the little lamp burning and Class 4 painted on the walls.

'Golly,' cried Christopher, looking round, 'you *are* a cartoonist, Scales! There's old Weef with his mouth open.'

'I don't have my mouth open,' protested Weefy, staring at his portrait with his mouth open.

'What a mucky drawing,' said Scales, smoothing out the sugar paper. 'What's it supposed to be?'

'It's for Cheer-up Monday,' they told him. 'We're trying to do a comic strip.'

'You want my silly cousins, if you want a comic strip,' said Scales. 'They

are a comic strip. Let's go and wake them.'

He took them up the secret way to the family cave, where the flat baking-rock was, and the fireplace. Then he went running up and down the bumpy wall, calling softly:

'Wake up, sillies, here's some of Class 4 to see you.'

Staring up from below, the boys saw, curled in crannies and crevices, cracks and corners, baby dragons fast asleep. Presently, bright little eyes and brisk little bodies came popping out of the shadows and twenty little dragons came scampering down with squeaks of pleasure.

'A wake-up in winter! What a surprise! Oh, it's Sam, oh, oh, it's clever Christopher, ooh, it's Weefy with his mouth open. Ooh, Scales, it's big Billy Bottom!'

'Hush, don't wake Grandrag, sillies,' hissed Scales. 'We're going out.'

'Outside in sleeptime?' squeaked the little dragons. 'Is the sun shining?'

'Of course it is,' growled Scales. 'Would I wake you, if it wasn't?'

Outside the cave a dazzling world of brilliant white made them blink and squeeze their eyes. The sky was as blue as Billy's eyes and a sharp blue shadow lay beside each snow-covered rock.

Scales began to boss. 'We'll have a Flying Glide. It's a sort of half run, half fly. I can't fly properly yet, because I've been hibernating and my muscles are weak. Sam, catch hold of the spike on the end of my tail, the others tag on behind. Sillies, tag on to Billy, biggest first, littlest last. Right. Are you ready? Here we go. YEEEEOW!'

The stinging air rushed past them.

'Hurray!' yelled the boys. 'Oooh!' squealed the cousins. It was like flying, it was like sliding, it was magic. They fetched up at the bottom in a tangle of boys and dragons, laughing their heads off.

'Oh, oh,' gasped Billy, 'that was fun. Look at Weef!'

Weefy was head down in the snow with his legs sticking up like the letter Y. Billy crunched over and pulled him out.

'Again,' cried all the little dragons. 'Oh, please, dear Scales, again.'

So Scales flutter-plodded up the mountain, carrying them all on his back, and they did it again, and again. But at the last time Billy said he didn't want to ride back, he wanted to walk.

'Because I'm going to make a snowball. The giantest snowball you ever saw.'

'And we won't ride on your back,' Sam told Scales, 'because you're puffed. We'll walk, too.'

So they started back, the boys laughing and joking as they panted along, and the little dragons jiggling and jostling as they changed places among Scales' spines. At the cave mouth, Scales shook himself, turned round and began to count his cousins.

'Fifteen,' he sighed, when he'd finished. 'So, where's the rest?'

He looked sternly at his cousins, who looked anxiously back at him. They didn't know where the rest of them were.

'They're hiding,' suggested one. 'Yes, yes, that's it. They're hiding,' cried another.

'In that case,' Scales told the boys,

'we'll soon find them. They're rotten hiders.'

So he and the boys began calling and searching, while the remaining cousins scuttered in front of them, crying, 'Look out, Scales is coming, Sam's getting warm, Weefy's boiling,' which didn't help.

Billy, pushing his enormous snowball up the mountain, thought, when I get to the top I'm going to let go and watch it go smash at the bottom. But when he got to the top, a better idea occurred to him. He heard Scales saying grimly:

'When I find these sillies, *I'll* hide them somewhere and forget where I hid them.'

Then Weefy's, 'Let's all shout, "We give up." Then they'll come out.'

Billy puffed on past them. Weefy, Sam and Christopher were gathered despondently round Scales, staring at their toes, their shoulders hunched. The five missing sillies were absolutely *no*where to be seen.

'I bet they're down at the bottom,' said Scales savagely.

There was a shout above them. Startled, they looked up. Poised on the edge of an overhanging rock immediately above them was an enormous snowball. Billy Bottom's pleased red face appeared round one side of it.

'Help,' cried Weefy as the snowball leant forward, fell, and flattened him. The little dragons laughed till their little sides blew in and out like bellows. Billy clapped his hands and danced on top of the rock. Scales opened his mouth to roar with rage when, out of the wreck of the giant snowball, crawled the five missing little dragons.

'Bless me!' cried Billy, staring down. 'They must have fallen off your back, Scales, and got rolled up in my snowball. I didn't see them, because I was behind pushing it.'

The sun went behind a cloud and the brightness vanished.

'Into the cave, everyone,' ordered
Scales, 'quicksticks and I'll blow you
dry.'

'Oh, what a ride we had,' squeaked
the five little dragons as Scales' warm
breath gusted over them. 'We went
rolypoly, rolypoly, rolypoly, rolypoly
up the mountain.' And they looked
at Billy Bottom with awe and
admiration.

'Now then,' said Scales to the boys
when the last cousin was dry, 'draw
what you saw and write what happened, and mind you put MY NAME
in the title, in caps, and *first*.'

He laughed and even Weefy felt
warm from top to toe, then the laugh

changed to a yawn and he blinked. 'Goodnight, see you in the spring.'

They felt themselves spiralling upwards on a warm thermal. Then they were in the bay and Miss Green was saying:

'You have worked hard. What a super comic strip. "SCALES and the Sillies and the Class 4 Four!" ' She began to read and laugh at the same time, but at the last picture, she suddenly stopped, looked round, and cried out:

'But where's Billy Bottom?'

5   Where IS Billy Bottom?

Indeed, where *was* Billy Bottom?

'Gone toilet?' suggested Sam, seeing Miss Green's bewildered face.

'Oh, go and look, please, Sam,' begged Miss Green.

But Billy was not in the toilet, not in the classroom, not in the playground, not in the library, *not* in the school.

'Oh, my goodness,' cried poor Miss

Green. 'Now, children,' she said, quickly, 'if any of you see Billy, or know where he may have gone, you must come and tell me or Miss Barley or Jenny at once. Billy hasn't been very happy lately and he may have run away.'

Then began a bustle and a babble: Miss Barley telephoning, Miss Green searching, Jenny the Helper running round to Billy's house, Class 4 calling, 'Billy, Billy, Billy,' and Mr Duffy and the Lollipop Lady clicking their tongues together.

'Oh, oh,' cried tiny Tina, 'to run *away*, from his *home*.'

'His mum's run away from it,' said Sam.

'You'd run away if you had Billy's brothers and his dad,' said Sebastian who was passing.

Mr Duffy left the Lollipop Lady and came down the passage.

'Mr Duffy,' cried Sam, 'do you know where Billy's gone?'

'Perhaps already he is ill and

dying,' said Tina, almost weeping.

'I doubt it,' said Mr Duffy. He leaned on his mop and addressed them. 'Billy's learnt *his* lessons *out* of school. He won't starve and he won't fall ill. There's no germ could get through his dirt.' (It was true Billy was never ill.)

'But he may,' began Sam, 'because he's not very . . .' He stopped. Billy was not very bright, but he didn't want to say that. It seemed disloyal.

'There's bright and bright,' said Mr Duffy, as if Sam had spoken, 'and there's Bottoms everywhere.' He passed on, clanking his pail.

'We must do something,' Tina said, bunching her tiny fists.

'We'll make up a search party after school,' declared Sam. He went up to Weefy Buffalo, who was sitting at Blue Table stitching the comic strip into the Cheer-up Book.

'Weef, we're going to make up a search party after school and search for Billy.'

'Why?' asked Weefy, who was always odd.

'Because he's lost,' cried Sam angrily.

'He's not,' said Weefy, pricking himself.

'He *is*,' said Sam. 'He has run away and . . .'

'He is cold and hungry and miserable,' finished Tina.

'He isn't,' said Weefy, watching a drop of blood come out of his finger. 'I bet he's warm and comfy and creasing himself.'

He put the drop of blood carefully on to one of the pictures and watched it spread and soak away.

'That's a disappointing red, for blood,' he remarked.

They banged him on the shoulders. 'Do you *know* where Billy is?'

'Yes.'

'Where?'

'In there.'

Weefy put his sucked finger on the last picture. In it Sam and Weefy and Christopher were walking away down Magic Mountain, waving goodbye to Scales, who was standing in the mouth of the cave waving back.

'Billy's not in the last picture!' exclaimed Sam.

''Course he isn't. He's stayed behind.'

'You mean *in* the cave? But I can't see him there,' said Sam. He and Tina stared at the drawing, but they could only see scribbles and blobs.

'He's probably crouching behind Scales,' said Weefy carelessly. 'Billy's always whizz at hiding. I'm going to Jenny to get a plaster.'

'Are you sure?'

'Positive, probably stuffing himself with rock-cakes,' and Weefy wandered off.

At hometime all the mums were talking about Billy's disappearance and none of them seemed surprised. Walking along Allotment Lane, Sam thought, how will he keep warm? Old cabbage stumps poked through the crumpled snow. Even the scarecrow looked frozen, and – where would Billy run *to*?

'Mum,' he said at teatime, 'Weef says Billy's in Scales' cave, warm and dry and eating rock-cakes.'

'That's wishful thinking,' said his mum. 'Weefy's enjoying a respite from Billy's bullying.'

'Billy doesn't bully him,' said Sam, surprised, 'and what's a respite?'

'A rest from something,' said his mother. 'Well, Billy was always shoving Weefy's face in the snow.'

'Only because Weefy didn't want him to,' said Sam.

His mother wouldn't let him go out to search for him, because it was too cold and dark.

'The police will be looking,' she said.

The next day there was no Billy and no news. Poor Miss Green looked ill and even Mr Duffy had his lips pursed. If Billy *is* on Magic Mountain, thought Sam, Miss Green ought to know. Playtime was indoors again; Weefy, whose turn it was to do the Weatherboard, had written 'AWFUL' on a piece of card and stuck it in. When the comics had been dished out and Miss Green had taken her handbag off to the staffroom, Sam and Tina slipped into the bay and crouched before the cave.

'Scales?' whispered Sam. '*Is* Billy with you? He's run away and we have to know.'

The cave was silent. Tina stretched her little arm in up to the elbow.

67

'I feel paper,' she whispered.

'You can't,' whispered Sam. 'Dinny and I swept it all out.'

'But I do and here it is,' and Tina pulled out a piece of torn sugar paper with Billy's sprawly, scrawly writing-drawing on it. It looked like this:

'Let's take it to Christopher,' said Sam. 'He will be able to decode it.' He was proud of the word 'decode'. Christopher had taught it to him.

'No,' said Tina stoutly, 'we found it, we will make it out, and if it is a message, we will take it to Miss Green.'

So together they puzzled over it.

'I think it's a drawing,' said Sam at last. 'I think that Y is Weefy stuck in the snow on Magic Mountain. The next bit is the cave. That's the sun, only it's funny he hasn't put rays round it. That lump must be trees or rocks. Then he's done another sun, why I don't know. Those squiggles must be the sillies and then . . . and then . . . more rocks?'

'Billy never does two suns in one picture and he always puts rays round them,' said Tina. 'And if he is drawing the Magic Mountain why has he drawn a boat and a fish? It is a very good boat and a very clear fish.'

'Billy always draws boats and fish, whatever the picture is,' said Sam, 'because he's good at boats and fish.'

'We will get his newsbook out and see how he does his writing,' decided Tina, frowning.

So they did and saw that some letters Billy got back to front, some wandered all over the page, and –

'Some he doesn't put in at all!' cried Sam.

'Now we can decode this drawing,' Tina said.

'This first letter *is* a Y, then there's an *a* back to front, then a fallen over *r*, then a poor *m* the wrong way round, the sun is an *o*, then a back-to-front *h* and a slipping *t* . . .'

'The next bit is "*to*",' cried Sam, catching on.

'The squiggles are not the Sillies, but "*see*" the wrong way round,' cried Tina, her pencil flying, 'and those aren't rocks, they're "*mi*" for "my".'

The last word baffled them. It was like a blown up bridge with a tele-graph pole leaning crazily against it. In the end they wrote down a *u* and an *n* and a kicking *k* and an *l*.

'Yar mo ht to see my un k l?' read Sam. 'What's it mean?'

But Tina was tugging him up and pulling him out of the classroom and running him up the corridor.

'Mr Duffy,' they cried, as they passed him in his cubby hole, 'we've found a message from Billy.'

Mr Duffy stretched out a long arm. 'Let's have a dekko then.'

'A dekko?'

'A look,' said Mr Duffy and took the sugar paper.

His eyebrows flew up. '*Yarmouth!*'

'But Yarmouth's miles away!' cried Sam.

'I don't suppose he's got there, but that's where he's heading,' grunted Mr Duffy, and his long legs raced their short ones to the staffroom.

Out came Miss Green, out came Miss Barley, out came a policeman, out came a lovely tracker dog, cleverer even than Christopher. The sugar paper went from hand to hand, and from hand to nose.

'Something to go on,' said the policeman and went smartly off.

'Of *course*, the Bottom boys have uncles *every*where,' sighed Miss Barley wearily.

'*Good* children,' praised Miss Green, 'oh, *good good* children.'

Everyone felt lighter, even the grey rain falling on the grey snow felt jolly.

Sam went bubbling home along the lane, dancing in the slushy snow, but next morning there was still no Billy and Miss Green looked white with

71

worry. By afternoon playtime she said:

'I think I'll stay in the classroom with you. Read us the Cheer-up Book, Sam, and cheer us all up.'

So Sam began reading the captions under the comic strip, but when he came to the last picture he gave a squawk of surprise.

'Billy's back!' he shouted, staring at the last picture, for there was Billy in it, walking down Magic Mountain with the others, waving to Scales, and, like an echo of his voice, 'Billy's back, Billy's back, Billy's back!' cried Class 4 all round him. Sam raised his head and saw Billy standing in the doorway shining like a sun.

'Billy,' cried Miss Green, leaping up, 'welcome back, and just look at you!'

For Billy had new trousers, new jumper, new shoes and *socks*! His hair was brushed, his face was clean, his *hands* were clean. He might have stepped straight out of a catalogue.

Sam cheered, Tina danced, Weefy stared.

'Oh, Billy,' laughed Miss Green, nearly crying, 'who bought you those lovely clothes?'

'My mum,' beamed Billy, nearly bursting. 'She's come home 'cause she missed me.'

He walked over to Weefy and threw his arms round him.

'Hi, Weef,' he said and wrestled him to the ground.

6 *THE Billy Bottom*

'Take your card out of the Weather-board, Weefy,' Miss Green said joyously, 'and put "Sunny" in. Who cares what the weather's doing? Billy's back and we *are* sunny.'

It was the afternoon of Billy's return and Magic Mat time.

'Please can Billy tell his run-away story?' asked Class 4.

'I don't want to tell it again,' said

74

Billy, who had already told it to the police, to Miss Barley, to his mum and to his dad. 'I want to tell a special bit I haven't told anyone yet.'

'I don't want to hear about running away,' said Miss Green, 'because running away is not a good thing to do, it's dangerous and nasty things can happen, but if you have a *happy* bit to tell us, do.'

'I have,' said Billy and he began.

'I was going across some fields where I'd been potato-picking with my mum, when it began to get foggy. It got whiter and whiter, and colder and colder, and I kept falling over, then I got leg-ache, then I got hungry.'

'Then you got frightened?' suggested Weefy.

'Then I did *not*,' said Billy stoutly. 'I shouted "Hi!" and a voice whispered, "Hi who?" So I shouted "Hi Billy Bottom" and the voice said, "*The* Billy Bottom?" and I shouted "Yes, but I'm lost," so the voice said,

75

"Give me your hand" so I put out my hand and a claw took it.'

Ivy Grubb screamed.

'*Then* you got frightened?' insisted Weefy.

'No, it was a nice claw. It pulled me up and up and up. Then the whiteness went and it was dark. Then the ground went hard instead of soggy and my voice echoed. The claw pulled me along and along till I saw a red glow and I was in a little round cave with a little red fire in a little round pot with holes in it, and an old, old dragon was looking from me to a picture on the wall beside her and the picture was *me*!'

Christopher cried out, 'The old 'un! Scales' grandmother!'

Billy nodded. 'She wasn't any bigger than my nan that died at Christmas. She was wrinkly and yellow and her spines were all fallen over. She had hardly any teeth and she said in a creaky, crackly voice, "So you're the Billy Bottom my grandson drew

for me?" ' Sam felt jealous. ' "Clatter the calling-stones and wake my grandson. It's a long, long time since a bold bully knight came seeking *me*."

'I saw a lot of flat stones hanging from the ceiling,' went on Billy, 'strung together on a boot-lace. So I clattered them and Scales came yawning in.

' "Oh, Grandrag, it's the middle of midnight," he said. Then he saw me. "Billy! How did you get here?"

' "He was in difficulties," said Grandrag, "so I pulled him up."

'Scales scowled. "It's *me* that

calls up Class 4, Grandrag, not you."

' "Jealousy is for knaves," said Grandrag, "fetch us a feast, grandson. I want to hear of the fights Billy's fought and the knaves he's knapped."

'So Scales went out and came back with a tray of –'

'Rock-cakes!' cried Class 4.

'Hardbake,' corrected Billy, 'and we ate and drank and I told Grandrag about our fights with the Class 1 gang –' ('When was that?' cried Miss Green, but Billy didn't heed her) ' – and the time I got Gripper down when he was kicking Weefy and the time I hit the Beetroot boy and Grandrag listened and laughed and beat her claws on the rock and called out: "I want a fight. I want to see if I can still breathe fire!"

' "She can't," Scales whispered to me, "but she loves fighting."

'So I took out my sword.'

'Your *sword*?' cried Class 4.

'My tin opener,' explained Billy.

'Your tin opener,' he said, seeing Sebastian's face, 'that I took with me in case I found a tin. Grandrag couldn't bite, because her teeth were loooo, and she couldn't see very well, but she was jolly quick on her turns. I was winning, when Scales, who'd been hopping about cheering us on, went suddenly quiet, and Grandrag stopped, and I stopped and looked round. Aunt Spiny was standing there, glaring.'

'*Oooh*,' said Class 4 on a long breath. Sam stopped feeling jealous and began to feel anxious.

'She looked at the jug and she looked at the plate and she looked at the picture, then she looked at Scales. Then she came up to me and snapped her teeth so close to my hair it lifted, and I jumped.

'"Just trying to take the night-cramps out of my legs, daughter," said Grandrag in a tiny voice. "Scales brought a friend along to help."

'Aunt Spiny said in a hissing, spitty

voice, "Little firstskin dragons do *not* take things out of the store cupboard without asking." And she hit Scales and he fell over. Then she said, "And old lastskin dragons should think of their digestions before they eat hardbake or joust with strange knights in the middle of midnight." And she helped Grandrag back to her sleeping place. Then she turned all her teeth on me and . . .'

Sam felt his heart clench and Class 4 held its breath.

'. . . took the tin opener out of my hand with her teeth, tossed up her head like this, and swallowed it!'

'But, but,' began Sebastian.

'It's all right,' Billy assured him. 'My mum's getting your mum a new one. Then Scales got up and said, "What were you doing when Grandrag helped you?" And I said, "Running away." And Grandrag cried out, "Oh, no, no, no, no, no, *The* Billy Bottom doesn't run away. My grandson's Billy Bottom's not a coward. *My* Sir William stands and fights!"

' "Now, Mother," Aunt Spiny said, "this boy wasn't running away. He was running *to* somewhere. Weren't you?"

' "I was going to Yarmouth," I told her, "only the fog came down and I got lost."

' "I thought so," she said, "you're not a boy for flight. Say goodnight to Grandrag."

81

'So I kissed Grandrag.'

'Ugh!' shuddered Ivy Grubb.

'Not ugh,' said Billy. 'She was soft and wrinkly like my nan that died at Christmas, and she smelt of hardbake. Aunt Spiny took Scales and me up to the big cave where Scales' mum was standing by the fire stirring.

' "Mum, can I take Billy to Yarmouth? He was going there, but there's fog on the fens," Scales asked.

' "You can take your grandmother her indigestion mixture," said his mum and gave him a bowl to carry. "I'll take Billy to Yarmouth, but first he must write a note to tell his parents where he's gone."

'Scales fetched a piece of paper, and I wrote a message and he said, "I'll put it in my Class 4 cave." '

'He did!' cried Tina. 'I found it!'

Billy looked pleased and Sam felt a glow of pride. Oh, *good* Scales, he thought, jolly, jolly good.

'Then,' went on Billy, 'Aunt Spiny and Scales went off to see to Grandrag and Scales' mum took me outside the cave. There wasn't any fog on Magic Mountain, just bright, bright stars. She picked me up in her front claws, spread her wings and . . .'

'Go on,' prompted Class 4, 'don't stop.'

'It gets mixed up,' Billy said slowly. 'First it was flying. Her claws were round me and I could hear her heart beating, thump, thump, thump. Then it was like riding in a lorry hearing the engine throbbing, but both times she was talking to me.'

'What was she saying?'

'She said, "You're going to be a big man, Billy. You'll be bigger than your brothers, bigger even than your Dad. Big enough to take on the world. And when you are, Billy . . ." Then I woke up and we were in Yarmouth and my uncle with the lorry was helping me down and my uncle with the fishing boat was standing on the quay and they were both talking to me, but I didn't answer because I was still listening.'

'Tell us,' said little Tina softly.

'She said, "And when you are, Billy, don't hit the world too hard." '

Class 4 sat silent, looking at him. Billy stared dreamily out of the window, where bigger and bigger patches of blue sky were appearing between the clouds.

'You've made it all up,' shouted Sebastian. 'You've lost our tin opener and you're making excuses.'

'You never were in that little cave,' Ivy Grubb said jealously. 'You never did see Scales' nan.'

Billy drew his hand slowly from his pocket. 'Oh, didn't I?' he retorted, and showed them a long yellow tooth, worn down, and very, very old.

'She broke it on the hardbake,' he said.

'What a lovely story, Billy,' said Miss Green, 'and you told it beautifully. How warm it is, children. Open the window, please, Billy.'

Billy seized the long window pole and opened the window, and a scent of violets stole in. A tortoise-shell butterfly woke up and began battering on the glass to get out.

'Someone's coming,' cried Tina, who was nearest the door.

The flower scents grew stronger, the air grew warmer, the sunlight poured in. Footsteps came along the corridor, and laughter.

'It's her,' cried Weefy suddenly. 'It's Per-sef!'

The door opened and Miss Barley pushed a little girl in. She was dressed in tunic and trousers embroidered all over with flowers and there were flowers in her hands. She came forward shyly and offered them to Miss Green.

'She'll be all right now,' said Miss Barley to someone behind her. 'Thank you, Miss Green.' Then she closed the door and went away.

It wasn't Persephone, nor yet Persef. It was Nargis Khan whose parents had taken the corner shop, but she brought the spring.

7 Newer Than New

The sun shone, the grass sprang, the daffodils shouted and the cuckoo came. In the classroom the coughs stopped and the spots began.

'We are a small class today,' said Miss Green, looking at her register.

'Poor old Weef's got chickenpox,' Sam said. 'He showed me his spots at his window this morning.'

'What we need is some fresh fen

air,' said Miss Green. 'I'll ask Miss Barley if we can go to the stream and get tadpoles.'

Miss Barley said yes and, presently, Class 4, looking more like a big family than a class, set out, wearing wellies and carrying jars. Jenny carried the First Aid Box and two changes of dry clothes. The mums who came to hear reading carried the lunch box and the lemonade. Miss Green carried a bucket because the tadpoles would want their own water to live in, and a book called *The Life of Stream and Pond.*

Soon they came to a flat brown stream between willows and began to search for tadpoles. Up they searched and down they searched till

S P L A S H !

'Oh, Sebastian,' cried Miss Green. 'I had a feeling the first dry clothes would be for you.'

She took off his wet clothes, rubbed him dry and hung his bow tie on a willow twig.

'My sister gave me that one,' stuttered Sebastian, struggling into dry clothes.

'It's very pretty,' said Miss Green.

'It's girlish,' said Sebastian.

'This is a real scientific tadpole search,' cried Christopher, wading lustily. 'Only thing is,' he added, 'there aren't any tadpoles.'

'Perhaps the melting snow made it too cold for them,' said Miss Green. 'We'll have lunch and try again.'

So they sat on a long willow branch and ate their lunch over the shallow stream. 'Now,' said Miss Green, 'some go upstream, some go down, but be gentle, be careful.'

'Be scientific,' said Christopher.

Sam moved off with Billy beside him, but Billy soon got bored.

'I'm going to climb trees,' said he and vanished.

The sun made the water look like melted toffee. The young willow shoots were golden, their new leaves glossy green. A poem shot into Sam's head.

Everything's new.
The sky is blue.
The willows are sway sway
   swaying.
Weefy's got spots,
Lots and lots.
I wish he was here and playing.

He had waded to a place where willows crowded into the water and the stream plaited itself over gravel banks. Kingcups and forget-me-nots bloomed, bright gold and gentle blue. Tiny fish darted on the bottom, but no tadpoles.

'Frog mums and dads
Where are your tads?
There should be shoals
Of fat, black poles.
Please send me some,
Frog dad and mum,'

sang Sam. The willows quivered as something pushed through them. The stream washed against his wellies as something plunged into it. The sunlight broke into a million gold pieces as it bounced off a hard, bright . . .

'Hello, Sam,' shouted Scales.

'Scales,' cried Sam, blinking, 'oh, Scales! *Gosh*, you're bright!'

'I'm new,' said Scales, admiring his reflection, 'I've got my second skin.'

'Do you slough it off like a snake?'
asked Sam.

'Good heavens, no. Snakes do
it every year. Dragons do it first
every seven years, then every fifty
years, then when they get as old as
Grandrag, every hundred years or
so.'

Sam could hardly look at him.
Scales was so bright.

'And you look so *strong*.'

'I am strong,' said Scales, swelling.
'I've been given three wishes. My dad
gave me one, my mum gave me one,
Aunt Spiny gave me one, so I've got
power.'

'So what will you wish for?' asked
Sam.

'I'm not going to wish for anything,' Scales said in surprise. 'I can
grant wishes. That's the power.'

'Golly,' said Sam, 'well, I wish I
could find tadpoles. We've come to
· get some and there aren't any.'

'Then scoop 'em up,' cried Scales
triumphantly, 'for there they are!'

'Yikes,' shouted Sam. 'Oh brill, oh ace, oh *mega*!'

He stooped and laid his jar on the bottom and a black cloud of tadpoles rushed into it.

'Scales,' he panted when he stood up. 'When Billy told about meeting Grandrag I was jealous. I'd like to meet her.'

'You shall,' said Scales. 'Leave your tads here. Put a stone on top of the jar and follow me.'

He pushed through the willows into a field where a grove of ancient willows leant together. They had grey trunks and silvery leaves and looked like wizards whispering secrets. Billy was sitting near them talking to a log.

'Hi, Billy,' called Sam. 'I've found tadpoles, millions of them.'

Billy and the log looked up. Billy's face split into a grin, and the tapering end of the log split open and showed a few yellow teeth leaning crookedly within.

'Grandrag,' cried Scales, bounding

up to the log, 'this is Sam. *My* Sam.'

'The famous Sam? Let me have a look at him. Help me, Sir William de Bottome,' wheezed the log.

Billy put his arm under what Sam had thought was a broken branch and lo! the twisted, bristly, log shape became a shrunken old she-dragon, rheumatically swishing her tail, and moving towards Sam unpleasantly fast.

Sam took a step backwards.

'Oho,' cackled Grandrag, her sunken eyes snapping, 'the great Sam is afraid. My Billy Bottom would never have stepped back.'

'Sam's not afraid,' cried Scales indignantly, 'are you, Sam?'

But Sam's heart was stuck in his throat and he couldn't speak. I wish I was brave, he wished desperately, and a new Sam leapt up inside him.

'Afraid?' shouted the new Sam. 'You just watch.'

He ran at Grandrag, seized her jaws

in his bare hands and tried to force them shut.

'Hurray,' shouted Billy. 'Don't hurt her, though.'

'Hurt me,' gasped Grandrag, flinging Sam off. 'A titchy, tiny boy hurt *me*!'

She beat her wings, the upper part of her body rose in the air. Her front claws reached for Sam. He ducked past her and leapt on her back. She humped him off and whirled to strike. Billy grabbed her wing and pulled her down. She rolled on him, pinning him underneath. Sam ran down her knobby back and jumped on her tail.

'Ouch,' yelled Grandrag and rolled

off Billy. She twirled her tail and Sam flew up. Her jaws swung round to get him. Billy grabbed her head. Scales danced about like a referee, shouting:

'Well done, Sam, oh, jolly good, Billy. Grandrag, that was a *foul*!'

Suddenly it was over. Grandrag sank down and lay like a log in the trampled grass. Her eyes closed, her mouth shut, her body was motionless.

'I've killed her,' gasped Sam.

A heavy-lidded eye like a piece of bark flickered. 'Don't boast,' hissed Grandrag. 'Knights never boast.'

She shook herself. Her scales rippled like grey water.

'That was as good as a massage. I feel as supple as a twoskin. I took you for a poltroon, Sam of the Rock, but I was wrong. You're no coward. What's this, what's this? Damsels, and another knight?'

Coming across the field towards them were Ivy Grubb, Tina, Nargis and Sebastian. The girls were wearing daisy chains and carrying a wreath of

forget-me-nots and kingcups. Without a tremor of fear, they put the wreath on Grandrag's head.

'We watched the fight,' they said. 'You beat the boys hollow, though it was two against one.'

Grandrag looked at Sebastian who was carrying his bow tie.

'I must fight you another day, Sir Knight,' she panted.

'I don't want to fight any day,' Sebastian assured her. 'I want to give you this.' And he offered her his bow tie.

'Buying me off, huh?' rasped Grandrag. She blew out a tiny red spark and a puff of smoke no bigger than a dandelion clock, but she looked at the bow tie with greedy eyes. Sebastian put it round her crest.

The girls clapped their hands. Billy cried out, 'That suits you.'

Grandrag beamed. 'Take me home the back way, grandson, so Spiny doesn't see us!' She waddled slowly off into the willow grove with Scales beside her. He called back over his shoulder:

'See you in the bay!'

'Children,' called Miss Green from the edge of the field.

They raced across to her. 'I've found tadpoles,' shouted Sam. 'Millions of them. I'll show you where.'

'We've seen Scales,' panted Billy.

'He'll be in the cave when we get back,' trumpeted Ivy.

'I saw two dragons,' laughed Nargis. 'A young one and an old one. We gave flowers to the old one.'

Miss Green looked startled. 'Oh!' she said. 'Did you?'

In the classroom they gathered round the Tadpole Table with the new glass tank on it, and Miss Green poured in her bucketful. Sam emptied his tadpoles in and the others emptied theirs.

'It's a shame old Weef isn't here,' said Billy.

'I wish he was,' said Sam.

'I am,' said Weefy, appearing through the archway. 'My spots aren't chicken-pox. The doctor came and he said they are an allergy like my hay fever. Have you seen Scales' cave? It's terrif.'

They crowded into the bay and stared with popping eyes.

'Oh, that *is* pretty,' said Miss Green. 'Someone with very dainty fingers has done that.'

The cave had been lifted on to the table and dusted. Tiny posies of flowers were stuck in the cracks and miniature moss gardens arranged on the lower slopes. Fresh sand and pebbles had been strewn before the mouth and the sand was scuffed as though Scales had just that moment gone in.

'It is spring on Magic Mountain,' smiled Nargis, who had very dainty fingers, 'and Scales is awake.'

'W-e-l-l,' said Miss Green. 'Scales isn't real, you know. Oh, my goodness,' she cried, staring at Sebastian, 'we've left your bow tie on the willow tree! I must go and get it in the dinner hour.'

'It's not there,' said Sebastian calmly. 'I gave it to Scales' nan. She liked it and I didn't.'

'You can't tell your mother a story like that, you silly boy,' said Miss Green. 'She'll never believe it!'

'She will,' said Sebastian. 'My mum's seen Scales.'

8 The Frighteners

'Weef's scared of the climbing frame,' laughed Christopher. 'He never goes to the top.'

'I'm afraid of falling,' admitted Weefy.

It was playtime. Class 4 had just had PE with the big apparatus. Now they were lying under the pink may-tree watching the baby class clamber over the outside playthings.

'They're not afraid,' said Sam.

'They're too young,' explained Weefy. 'You get more frightened as you get older. I'd *like* to be brave.'

'I'll teach you to be brave,' said Scales. All looked up. Scales was in the maytree, woven comfortably in and out of the thorny branches, not minding the spikes a bit. He reached down and hauled them up one by one. There was a scratchy feeling, a tangly feeling, then –

'Here we are,' cried Scales cheerfully. 'Spring on Magic Mountain!'

'What a difference from last time!' cried Christopher for the air was clear and tangy, the short turf sparkled with flowers, and the rocks were brilliant with lichen.

'Now then, here's Frightener Number One,' cried Scales. 'Who's going to face it?'

All turned and saw with a gasp a nasty-looking creature lifting itself above a rock. Christopher pulled out his pad and pencil and rushed up to it.

102

'Oh, be careful,' cried Tina, as the Frightener opened a vast mouth bristling with teeth.

'It's got three rows of teeth like a shark,' cried Christopher, 'and a forked tongue like a snake.' He began to draw frantically. 'Hang on, hang on, don't swallow me yet. I want to draw your mouth. Oh, don't shut it up, *don't* shut it.'

But the big mouth shut sulkily. Stealthily, the Frightener uncurled two terrible talons.

'Look out,' screamed Class 4, 'it's going to tear you in bits, Chris!'

'Thanks,' shouted Christopher dodging about as the Frightener clawed at him. 'Wait a bit, wait a bit, *two* curved talons on each – what are they, hands or paws, do you know?'

The Frightener stopped and looked at them. Then it shook its head and blew steam at Christopher.

'Stop steaming,' commanded Christopher crossly, 'you're making

my paper damp. You're so *interesting*, I'm going to get you all down.'

But the Frightener humped away.

'He won't come back,' laughed Scales. 'Frighteners like frightening. They can't stand being analysed.'

'What's that mean?' Sam asked.

'Being discussed,' said Christopher, 'taken to pieces, understood.'

'Come on,' said Scales, 'let's find another one.'

He whisked ahead. Class 4 followed in a mixture of feelings, joy at the loveliness of everything, excitement at the adventure and fear at what might happen.

'A-a-a-a-h!' they screamed, piling up against each other.

A huge Frightener barred their way. 'I'm going to eat you up s-l-o-w-l-y,' it grinned, 'beginning with – YOU.' And it lunged at Billy Bottom.

There was no time to scream or offer advice. Billy put down his bullet head and struck it straight in the stomach. *Phuttt*! went the Frightener as all the air rushed out of it. Over it went, Billy with it, head-over-heeling down the mountain from rock to rock to rock. Class 4 and Scales went leaping after them. They found both at the bottom in a nest of flowers, Billy with one eye turning purple and his upper lip puffing out. They peeled him off the Frightener, who was underneath, and it crawled away, crushed.

'That's one way to get rid of them,' said Scales. 'Tough, but it works.'

'Silly, rough boys,' scoffed Ivy Grubb, tossing her ringlets, and she and Nargis and Dinny and Tina went skipping on ahead, picking flowers and singing, when –

G-r-r-h! A-a-a-r-g-h!! R-O-A-R!!!

Six scary Frighteners came striding towards them.

'Oh, oh! Oh no! Oh my!' cried Tina, Nargis and Dinny, but Ivy, after one astonished stare, marched up to the Frighteners and said, shaking her finger furiously:

'Go *away*, you stupid, stupid, stupid, stupid, *stupid* things. You don't frighten *me*!'

'Nor me,' shouted Dinny, her red pigtails bristling, 'you squashed, fat, ugly things.'

'Go home,' blazed Tina, black eyes flashing, 'go and help your mothers do the washing.'

'Take your feet off the flowers,' shrilled Nargis. 'Can't you do anything except crush and spoil?'

Their scolding rose up round the

Frighteners like a flock of whirling birds. The Frighteners bunched together, trembling, then turned and ran.

'What a racket you girls were making,' said the boys, coming up. 'It made us feel sorry for the Frighteners.'

'Huh!' snorted the girls and they linked arms and marched ahead, tossing their plaits and pony-tails.

'What will you do if you meet a Frightener?' Sam asked Weefy.

'Run,' said Weefy, and just then he met one. It leapt at him hissing like a kettle.

'Yipes,' squealed Weefy and ran like a hare.

Grinning with glee, the Frightener ran after him, but Weefy was faster. His sparrow legs flashed through the flowers, his mouth, always open, took in great gulps of air, his skinny arms drove his light body forward like pistons.

'He'll beat him,' cried Christopher.

'Go it, Weefy,' yelled Class 4,

panting after him. But the Frightener was gaining, growing bigger with every pace and roaring with triumph. Then a different roar filled the air. A waterfall appeared, hurling itself down the rocks to a foaming pool below.

'Run,' screamed Class 4 as the Frightener pounded up to Weefy.

'Got you!' roared the Frightener and leapt. Weefy looked back, shrieked, tripped and fell. The Frightener hurtled over him splash into the pool. Class 4 reached Weefy and picked him up. The Frightener rose spluttering through the white water, glugging and gargling.

'Oh, oh, oh! Look – look – look at it! *Oh*, how funny,' cackled Class 4.

The Frightener hauled itself out and sat by Weefy with the water pouring from it. It had shrunk and when it spoke, its voice had shrunk too.

'That wasn't fair,' it whispered. 'I didn't know you were going to do that.'

'Neither did I,' said Weefy honestly. 'It was an accident.'

Sam turned to grin at Scales who was watching from a tall rock and saw something cruel and coily come dangling down towards Scales from a ledge above.

A Frightener, and what a Frightener! It lifted its wicked head and looked at him and he felt his blood turn to ice. He couldn't move, he couldn't speak. It's my Frightener, he thought, it's going to kill me. Then he saw the Frightener dart its head down towards Scales and his brain said, it's going to kill Scales! My *friend*! His legs ran forward, his voice shouted:

'Scales, behind you!'

Scales whipped round. The Frightener drew back, hissing. Sam flung himself up the rockface and stood shaking by Scales. The Frightener had shrivelled to a black streak and they saw it slithering away.

'Oh, Sam, you saved my life. He's the worst Frightener. I'll tell my dad and he'll sort him out.'

'I'll sort him out,' gritted Sam, and felt himself burn with rage. 'If he touches *you*.'

Down below Weefy was having a conversation with his Frightener.

'You're not making friends with a *Frightener*, are you?' sneered Christopher.

'I am so, too,' said Weefy, 'he's interesting.'

'There are some you can make small,' said Scales, coming up, 'but you have to watch they don't start getting big again. Now then, heroes and heroines, time to go back.'

He led them down the mountain, following the stream that flowed from the pool.

'Cross here by these stepping stones.'

'Not the middle one,' whispered Weefy's Frightener.

'Righto,' said Weefy and jumped over it to the next stone.

'Coward,' jeered Christopher and stepped on to it. The stone tilted, he wobbled, Weefy reached back and saved him just in time.

'Up the tree now,' called Scales.

'Not on that branch,' murmured Weefy's Frightener. Weefy paused, and tested it. It broke in a cloud of dust.

'Hurry, hurry, hurry,' whimpered his Frightener. Weefy hurried.

Through the tangles, through the scratches and down on to the bare patch beneath the maytree. The baby class had gone in. The playground was empty. A cross Miss Green was coming towards them with the bell in her hand and a frown on her face.

'Ooh, we never heard the bell,' whispered Class 4. 'We're in trouble.'

They were, too, but Weefy wasn't. He was in the classroom, getting out his books.

9 Ivy to the Rescue

'What I like best,' said Weefy, 'is sprinkling the flour on.'

'What I like best is rolling it out,' said Billy Bottom, thumping away with his rolling pin.

'Silly rough boys,' sniffed Ivy, 'your pastry will be as heavy as lead.'

They were cooking, the boys in blue aprons, the girls in green.

'Now,' said Mrs Beeston, who

taught cooking, 'while the tarts are cooking, write out the recipe,' and she gave them paper and pencil.

But they'd been concentrating long enough, and standing too, and nobody finished copying out the recipe except Ivy, who always finished what she began.

'That's good, Ivy,' approved Mrs Beeston. 'Now you'll know how to make pastry whenever you want to.'

The tarts began to smell and she took them out. Some were burnt and some were tough and most weren't round at all, but Ivy's were round and frilly and a delicate gold, and her jam, neatly blobbed in the middle, shone like rubies.

They went back to the classroom with their tins.

'Stay in the bay for a bit,' called Miss Green, who was hearing reading. 'It's not long till belltime.'

The bay was full of sunshine – Scales came out of his cave. 'What's that glorious smell?'

'Jam tarts,' they said and opened their tins, six tarts and a recipe in each.

'Have one, dear Scales,' said tiny Tina, offering her tin.

'Let's all have one,' suggested Billy.

'A picnic in the bay,' cried Ivy.

'A picnic on Magic Mountain,' shouted Scales.

'Less noise in the bay there,' called Miss Green, but they never heard her, because they were standing on Magic Mountain with flowers at their feet and a view of the valley below them.

'That was quick, Scales,' said Sam. 'You're getting cleverer.'

'I've always been clever,' said Scales. 'I was in a hurry, that's all.

We'll have the picnic down here, because if we go up to the cave we'll have to share with my silly cousins, and that will mean only one and a half and a bit tarts each.'

'This is a super spot,' cried Sam. 'I can see a town with a wall round it and a river running past it to the sea.'

'And a big gate with people coming out of it like a football crowd,' cried Billy. 'Only not jolly.'

'Not jolly at all,' little Tina said, 'sad, very sad.'

'They are leading a girl,' cried Nargis suddenly.

'She's very bendy and droopy,' remarked Weefy.

A horrible thought came into Sam's heart. 'Scales, it's not, it's not . . . ?'

'Yes, it is,' said Scales, bending over the tarts, 'it's Maiden Devouring Day. My dad'll be there presently.'

'To *eat* her?' cried Nargis in horror.

'Oh, not *your* dad, dear Scales?' pleaded Tina.

But Ivy snapped, 'We must rescue her *now*!'

The boys hesitated. Frighteners were one thing, but – Scales' *dad*?

'I've got to stay on the mountain to keep watch in case any of the knights come fooling up, knowing my dad's down there,' Scales told them. 'The Princess doesn't feel anything,' he said to the girls, 'it's too quick.'

'How do you know?' retorted Ivy. 'You've never been swallowed. Are you boys coming or aren't you?'

'I'm not,' said Weefy, 'too dangerous.'

'I'm going down to watch it,' Billy said. 'I want to see Scales' dad.'

'Well, we're not picnicking with you lot,' stamped Ivy furiously. 'Come on, girls, we'll leave these wimps and wallies.'

The girls snatched up their tins and stalked off. Scales called after them, 'Go and play with my cousins, they're in the cave.'

Billy began running down the mountain. 'Go with him, Sam,' said Scales. 'My dad's very improooivc. He comes swimming in from the sea. And it's only *one* Princess *once* a year and the swallowing's over in a second.'

So Sam, with a troubled mind, went running down after Billy, and Weefy after him, prudently carrying his tin and Billy's. They came to the river bank in time to see a boat put out from the opposite shore with the Princess in it. Two men rowed it to a rocky islet and chained her to a little cliff facing the sea. Then they rowed back, leaving the Princess staring glumly out to sea with her lemony hair twirling on her shoulders.

If only we had guns, thought Sam, or a helicopter or a submarine. The townspeople on the opposite bank were all staring towards the river-mouth, but further up on the same

bank some women were washing clothes at the water's edge, their donkey carts tethered behind them, as though nothing unusual was happening.

Suddenly, a boat came scooting down river paddled by Ivy, Tina and Nargis, their biscuit tins shining in the bottom. They drove in among the washerwomen, Tina and Nargis jumped out and the boys heard Ivy's bossy voice and saw her point. One of the washerwomen flung a sheet at her, got in, and rowed the boat across to the back of the islet with strong, sweeping strokes. Ivy got out clutching the sheet. Then, one after the other, out came –

'Scales' silly cousins,' gasped the boys, their eyes popping.

Round the rock teetered Ivy in her shiny shoes and round the rock ran the little dragons.

'They're biting the Princess's chains off,' Weefy shouted.

'Shut up,' hissed Sam, 'the soldiers will hear you.'

But the soldiers were watching the river-mouth.

'Must be pretty weak chains,' muttered Billy. Perhaps they were. Anyway they fell off. Ivy hustled the Princess away. The little dragons bunched and scattered into a sort of pattern and Ivy draped the sheet over them. Some caught it in their teeth and pulled it over them, and there was a drooping white Princess-shape huddled against the cliff.

'It's like watching Match of the Day without close-ups,' laughed Billy. 'But what if the soldiers look now?'

Ivy was hustling the Princess round the islet and into the boat, where the washerwoman covered her up with an old shawl. She rowed sharply back to the shore, where the other women were listening to Tina and Nargis reading to them from a paper they held in their hands. The minute the boat touched the shore everybody bundled into the donkey carts and went trotting down the road as if their houses were on fire.

'Golly, that was quick,' cried Billy. 'They've gone through the gates into the town and no one noticed.'

'Might as well sit down then,' said Weefy.

So they sat down, and it was pleasant on the river bank. The water danced. The sun shone. They even dozed a little.

Then a great sigh, that was half a groan, yet with excitement in it, came from the crowd, and, sitting up, they saw a white bow wave speeding up the river and behind it

S C A L E S ' D A D .

'Whew! he's *big*,' breathed Billy, who was a judge of bigness.

'But he'll eat the sillies,' cried Sam, dancing with anxiety, 'he'll swallow them by mistake. Oh, Mr Scales, Mr Scales, don't . . .'

But his voice was drowned by the slap of the wave on the rock and the roar that broke from Scales' dad as the wave sucked the sheet and the little dragons into the water.

'WHERE'S MY PRINCESS?'

'Here,' cried a bold voice, and shooting out from the town water-gate came a long boat rowed by six washerwomen, with Ivy, Tina and Nargis in the middle holding a long, wide, flattish parcel covered in a white sheet.

Right under the nose of Scales' affronted Dad they drove the boat. The girls jumped out and, helped by the women, lugged the parcel up the rock and stood it against the little cliff.

'There's your Princess,' said Ivy scornfully. 'Eat *her*.' And whipped away the sheet.

'Oooh,' sighed the crowd for – *what* a princess! A lemony, curranty, sugary, spicy, cinnamony, shining golden brown princess with a flaked almond smile, apple ring eyes and two stiff plaits with lemon peel bows.

Scales' Dad stared, sniffed, licked and – down in one swallow? No! She was too good for that. He chewed, tasted, nibbled, savoured, and when he had finished, he turned to the townsfolk and roared:

'Make me a pastry princess every year and NO MORE GIRLS!'

The little dragons who had been bobbing about climbed carefully up him, the crowd cheered and he swam slowly, majestically, happily on up the river. The long boat dropped the girls off on the boys' side, and they came smugly up, holding their tins with the lids firmly on. There was a shout from Scales, and Sam's tin came rolling down to him.

'See you later, must get home in case Dad scolds the sillies. Back you go.'

'Now then,' said Miss Green's voice, 'let's have a look at your jam tarts.'

They blinked. They were back in the bay, the sun hot on their necks, standing with their tins in their hands, with Miss Green looking at them.

'Well done, girls, your mums and dads *are* going to have a treat at teatime. Ivy, you are a champion pastrycook! Out you go to play. Now, boys, let's have a look at yours. Oh, *boys* . . .'

With a start the boys followed her indignant gaze and saw that their tins were empty. Not a single jam tart remained. Somewhere, some time, they had eaten the lot.

10 Goodbye, Miss Green

'First the good news,' smiled Miss Green, pink as a rose. 'I'm getting married at Easter.'

'I know,' cried Sebastian, 'because my mum's making . . .'

'I know you know, Sebastian, and you've been very good not to tell. Now the bad news. I am *not* letting Scales into next term.'

'That's not fair! That's *mean*,'

stormed Class 4.

'It is fair and I'm lovely,' retorted Miss Green. 'Scales wasn't meant to be in this term, remember?'

It was three days to the end of term. Class 4 were making Easter baskets for the Easter Bunny to put Easter eggs in, one per basket, on the last morning of term.

'Miss has left it till now to tell us, because she knew we'd moan,' whispered Billy whose Easter Basket looked like an Easter road crash.

'What shall we call you next term?' asked Ivy, but Miss Green only looked mysterious.

'Wait and see,' she said.

'We *can't* say goodbye to Scales,' grieved Sam to Christopher. 'I'd sooner say goodbye to Miss Green.' And he felt hollow, because he liked Miss Green.

'We'll consult a book,' decided Christopher, 'because books are where you get ideas from.'

In the slack few minutes before

129

dinner, they went to the library and scanned the shelves. 'This one,' said Christopher, pulling a book out and finding a page. 'You ask her to read it at Magic Mat time.'

So at Magic Mat time, Sam handed the book to Miss Green and said, 'Please, will you read us this one,' and Miss Green said, 'Yes,' and read it.

'Poor Rumpelstiltskin,' said little Tina, 'that must have hurt, tearing himself in half.'

'That's just the storyteller's way of telling us how furious he was,' comforted Miss Green.

'That story's like "Tom Tit Tot",' remarked Dinny.

'Yes, it is,' agreed Miss Green. 'Names have always been magic. If you could guess somebody's name, you had power over them.'

'Miss Green,' said Christopher cleverly, 'if we guess your married name, will you let Scales into summer?'

Class 4 began to bounce and clap.

'Yes, yes,' they shouted. 'A guessing game. Yes!'

Miss Green looked at them all, her eyes full of smiles.

'All right, but first, two rules. You may only guess at Magic Mat time, and on the last morning of term *before* the Easter Bunny comes.'

'Right,' said Christopher swiftly. 'Is he Mr Wood?'

'No,' said Miss Green.

'Mr Tree, Mr Bush, Mr Leaf, Mr Root?' guessed Class 4, the idea sparking from mind to mind like an electric current.

'He is not a forest,' said Miss Green.

'Mr Gold, Mr Silver, Mr Steel, Mr Copper?'

'He is not a metal.'

'Mr Rivers, Mr Lake, Mr Brook, Mr Waters?'

'He is not wet,' said Miss Green coldly.

'Mr Brown, Mr Black, Mr White, Mr Grey, Mr Blue, Mr –?'

'There's the bell,' said Miss Green quickly, 'and he was none of those.'

Class 4 went out buzzing. 'We must be scientific,' said Christopher. 'Let's take it alphabetically. Sam, *you* think of all the names beginning with *a*, Billy, you think of all the names beginning with *b* . . .'

Next day they fired away. 'Mr Able, Mr Bonny, Mr Candy, Mr Dear . . .?'

'He is all those,' smiled Miss Green, 'but they are not his names.'

'Do you think we won't guess it?' asked Christopher, watching her face.

'I know you won't,' she laughed. 'It's so funny.'

'Oh! Mr Jokes, Mr Trix, Mr Poopiboo, Mr Baked Beans?'

'Not that sort of funny. Odd, strange.'

'Oh, then Mr Strange? Mr Odd? Mr Oddy?'

'Not that sort of strange, and there's the bell.'

'Only one more Magic Mat time,' groaned Sam, as they went out.

Class 4 grew cunning. Sebastian met Miss Barley in the corridor. 'Miss Barley, do you know what Miss Green's married name will be?' he asked, but 'My lips are sealed,' said Miss Barley, and walked on.

'We're trying to guess Miss Green's married name,' Ivy told Mrs Beeston.

'Mr Why-Can't-You-Cook-Like-My-Mum no doubt,' sniffed Mrs Beeston.

Sam found Mr Duffy in his cubby hole. 'Mr Duffy, what do you call the

133

man who's going to marry Miss Green?'

'Lucky,' said Mr Duffy.

'I mean, do you know his name?'

'I know his first, it's Alan.'

'Alan who?'

'I didn't hear any more,' said Mr Duffy. 'She just said "Alan" and kissed him.'

The next day Christopher brought a long list of all the surnames in his family, in the street and in the neighbourhood. Miss Green looked at it and laughed.

'It isn't anyone in East Anglia.'

Class 4 began asking parents, but the parents were silly.

'Prince Edward, Boris Becker, Terry Wogan,' they said.

'Terry Wogan's *married*,' Class 4 said in disgust.

The last Magic Mat time came. Class 4 guessed and guessed, but to all their guesses, Miss Green said, 'No.' When the bell went, she waltzed into the bay and did a little dance before Scales' cave, singing:

'If by tomorrow I still say no
Into the dustbin you shall go.'

'You haven't won yet,' cried Class 4. 'We've still got tomorrow morning before the Easter Bunny comes.'

'The Easter Bunny gets up very early,' laughed Miss Green, 'earlier than you do.' And she went twirling home.

But on the morrow it seemed that the Easter Bunny had not got up at all, because the Easter Baskets were eggless.

'Ha!' said clever Christopher. 'Our eco-system's broken down.'

'There's been a muddle at the Cash-and-Carry,' said Sebastian. 'That's where they get the eggs from.'

'They do not,' said Tina indignantly. 'The Easter Bunny brings them.'

'More guessing time, anyway,' said Weefy. 'Is it a hyphenated name, Miss Green? You know, two names with a little dash between them?'

'It is not,' said Miss Green, 'and I'm not giving you any clues. You're not the baby class. You were warm once, but not now.'

Sam wandered away into the bay. He had guessed so many names that even his own sounded made up. He put his arms round Scales' cave and laid his head on it.

'Oh, Scales, if we can't guess her married name, she's going to put your cave in the dustbin.'

'Let her,' came Scales' voice, sounding muffled. 'Who wants a cave in summer?'

Sam raised his head, astonished. His arms were full of Scales, and he was sitting on Magic Mountain, hugging him. Between Scales' spines, he could see a long eared figure hopping along hastily with a bundle on its back.

'That batty rabbit,' smiled Scales, 'he forgot the eggs! My silly cousins have been up since dawn making them. You should see some of them.'

'Scales,' cried Sam, thumping him, 'you won't *be* in next term, because we can't guess Miss Green's new name.'

'She won't have a new name,' scoffed Scales. 'She'll have the same name, only different, same as when I change my skin.'

'But she's going from a Miss to a *Mrs*,' shouted Sam.

'Well, that'll be the difference, *Mrs* Green,' said Scales, carelessly.

Sam jumped, and, thud, his feet landed in the bay. Class 4 were going through the door in two lines and Miss Green was coming through the archway to fetch him.

'Quick, Sam, Miss Barley wants everyone in the hall for a few minutes.'

'Next term I'll say *Mrs* Green,' cried Sam, looking at her.

Miss Green gasped and clutched herself. 'Don't tear yourself in half,' begged Sam, alarmed. 'It was Scales who guessed.'

When they came back from the hall, after Miss Barley had told them to help their mothers in the holidays and not to go with strangers, there was an egg in each basket – odd-looking eggs, a bit lumpy, but delicious – and on Miss Green's desk a big, perfectly-shaped one.

'I bet Scales made that one,' said Sam.

'Oh, Sam, Sam, you and Scales,' sighed Miss Green, then, 'Listen, Class, Sam has guessed my married name, so Scales' cave can stay. Tell them, Sam.'

So Sam told them, Class 4 cheered, and Scales' cave was put under his table in the bay, because, as Miss Green said, 'There may be a chilly night or two in the summer.'

At hometime, Sam put his Easter Basket into his bag and went into the bay.

'You were right, Scales, she's going to marry a *Mr* Green, so you will be here next term.'

'Of course I will,' said Scales sleepily. 'I don't know why you ever doubted.'

He was lying in a pool of sunlight, the warmth bouncing off him. Sam laughed with joy, oh, the dusty lanes of summer and the days that never end.

'*Summer*, Scales!'

'Summer, Sam.'

THE END

DRAGON IN CLASS 4

by June Counsel
illustrated by Jill Bennett

One morning on his way to school Sam rescues a young dragon trapped in the chains of a swing. Scales – as the dragon is called – decides to join Class 4 and he brings lots of fun to Sam and his friends.

Scales becomes Sam's special friend and he helps him with his spelling and in fighting off the school bully.

'Don't worry, I'll look after you,' says the dragon. 'I've always wanted a boy of my own!'

An amusing and lively fantasy for young readers.

0 552 52313 5

CORGI YEARLING BOOKS

A DRAGON IN SUMMER

by June Counsel

'Summer term, Sam,' Scales beamed, *'and I'm in it!'*

Sam bounces back to school for the Summer term, looking forward to seeing his special friend Scales again. But will Scales, a young dragon, *want* to be in the term when he hears that Sam's class are going to act out a pageant of St George and the Dragon – and the dragon gets killed?

Luckily Scales knows the story of St George too, although *his* story has a very different ending, and he is determined to share in the fun. Soon Scales is right in the middle of all the excitement, bringing his silly little cousins along to watch the pageant, and whisking Sam and his friends off to Wish Wood and an enchanted island for a series of super adventures!

'A delight of lords and ladies, dragons and castles, witches and magic . . . highly recommended' *Recent Children's Fiction*

0 440 86294 9

CORGI YEARLING BOOKS

DRAGON IN TOP CLASS

by June Counsel

Sam and his friends are in Top Class – and that means lots of exciting new things to learn. Especially Science, and when Top Class begin to learn about Flight, Scales – the young dragon who is Sam's special friend – whisks them off for a wonderful, whirling fantasy adventure on Magic Mountain. Can Top Class save the mountain from a greedy king? Break a spell on the Magician's daughter? And can Scales *really* do the impossible? They only know one thing for sure: Top Class is . . . top fun!

'Rollicking stories . . . will make every young reader wish to be a member of Top Class' *The Junior Bookshelf*

0 440 86321 X

CORGI YEARLING BOOKS

A SELECTED LIST OF TITLES
AVAILABLE FROM CORGI YEARLING
BOOKS

THE PRICES SHOWN BELOW WERE CORRECT AT THE TIME OF
GOING TO PRESS. HOWEVER TRANSWORLD PUBLISHERS
RESERVE THE RIGHT TO SHOW NEW RETAIL PRICES ON
COVERS WHICH MAY DIFFER FROM THOSE PREVIOUSLY
ADVERTISED IN THE TEXT OR ELSEWHERE.

☐ 0 440 86293 0   **THE KEEP-FIT CANARIES**   *Jonathan Allen* £2.99

☐ 0 440 86294 9   **A DRAGON IN SUMMER**   *June Counsel* £2.50

☐ 0 440 86267 1   **DRAGON IN CLASS 4**   *June Counsel* £2.99

☐ 0 440 86321 X   **DRAGON IN TOP CLASS**   *June Counsel* £2.99

☐ 0 440 86332 5   **TABBY'S C.A.T.**   *Stan Cullimore* £2.99

☐ 0 440 86314 7   **THE GENIE OF THE LAMPPOST**   *Rachel Dixon* £2.99

☐ 0 440 86323 6   **EATING ICE CREAM WITH A WEREWOLF**   *Phyllis Green* £2.99

☐ 0 440 86340 6   **HARRIET'S HARE**   *Dick King-Smith* £2.99

☐ 0 440 86277 9   **SHRUBBERY SKULDUGGERY**   *Rebecca Lisle* £2.50

☐ 0 440 86325 2   **THE WEATHERSTONE ELEVEN**   *Rebecca Lisle* £2.99

☐ 0 440 86337 6   **FINDERS KEEPERS**   *Rebecca Lisle* £2.99

☐ 0 440 86312 0   **GERALD AND THE PELICAN**   *Caroline Pitcher* £2.99

☐ 0 440 86262 0   **ROBBIE AND THE GANGSTERS**   *Victoria Whitehead* £2.99

☐ 0 440 86231 0   **GLUBBSLYME**   *Jacqueline Wilson* £2.99